# HOCKEY WARS

**SAM LAWRENCE & BEN JACKSON**

www.indiepublishinggroup.com

ISBN: 978-1-988656-24-3 Paperback

ISBN: 978-1-988656-25-0 Hardcover

Editor: Matthew Godden

*This book holds a special place in my heart. I want to thank my Mom & Dad for giving up so much so I could play hockey when I was growing up.*

—Sam

# 1

"PLEASE BE HERE," Millie begged. "Please be here."

She dumped the entire contents of her backpack onto her bed, but doing so only confirmed her suspicion. Her homework was nowhere to be found.

She stared down at the mess and took a moment to contemplate her options: She could either run back to school and retrieve the assignment to avoid her mother's wrath, or she could make up a lie about not having homework and meet her friends at the pond before the boys showed up.

It really wasn't much of a choice. Her parents had a "talk" with her when she turned ten about keeping her grades up if she wanted to keep up all the sports. Millie was struggling with her grades as it was, and if she got anything less than a B on her next report card, her parents would flip out and ban her from playing hockey for sure.

Talk about cruel and unusual punishment.

Sighing, Millie slung her empty backpack back over her shoulder and ran downstairs, taking the steps two at a time. Her school was less than five minutes away from her house, but right now, those five minutes might as well have been five hours.

First, she would have to find her homework in her mess of a desk, then return home to grab her gear before finally making her way over to the frozen pond in the woods behind old Mrs. Jefferson's house. The pond was the only place in town to skate and practice hockey other than the local rec center, which cost money and required you to have parental supervision. Chances were that by the time Millie got there, it'd already be too late for her team to stake their rightful claim.

*Ugh.* She could already picture Cameron's smug face; not to mention her teammates'. They were gonna be so ticked off when she didn't show up right away. They'd been looking forward to the extra practice time all weekend.

Now, the casual observer might have accused Millie of being overly dramatic, but in the small town of Dakota, hockey wasn't just a game. It was a way of life. Pretty much everyone either played hockey or supported their friends and family who did. That was why their beloved pond was decked out with two nets, and a tiny fence that served as boards. It was a sweet setup, but it also came with a strict set of rules—the main one being, first come, first play.

Back in the days when all the Dakota fourth graders had played on the same team, this rule had never been a problem. Everyone in town knew that from four to six on school days, the ice belonged to the Lightning.

However, about two years ago everything had changed. Millie and seven of her closest friends had split from the Lightning to form their own team, the all female Dakota

Hurricanes, and just like any two good hockey teams from the same town, the Lightning and the Hurricanes had a bitter rivalry, especially between the two captains.

The ironic part was that before the split, Cameron and Millie hadn't hated each other at all. They'd actually been best friends. Heck, they were practically siblings. They'd grown up together, just as their parents had before them, and because of this, they knew exactly what to say to push each other's buttons. It made the daily battle for the pond super intense.

Like, more intense than a shootout, even.

It also didn't help that the teams were evenly matched in just about every way, right down to there being eight of the best players from each team in the same class at Dakota Public School. It made game days pretty awkward, as the non-hockey-playing students were forced to pick sides when they played exhibition games against each other.

If Millie was being honest with herself, she did feel a little bit bad about that. But only a little. She and her friends had their reasons for starting their own team, and it was great being able to hang out and practice and not have to worry about anyone teasing you for being a girl or telling you to take up figure skating instead of hockey. Not that she thought her former teammates had actually meant any of those comments, but they still hurt.

As far as the rivalry went, though, that was mostly on Cameron. He was always the first one to start slinging insults and take things to a mean and nasty place. Knowing him, he was probably already at the pond making fun of Georgia's small size and Ashlyn's missing tooth, as if he didn't have plenty of missing teeth himself.

The thought made Millie scowl and clench her fists, but there was nothing she could do at the moment. She just had to hurry up and hope for the best.

"So, where's your fearless leader?" Cameron asked, looking down at Georgia with a superior grin.

The girls were dressed in full gear, standing with their arms crossed at center ice. The boys of the Lighting outnumbered them by one, and they weren't very impressed by the display.

"She'll be here," Georgia said threateningly—well, as threateningly as a four foot three, ten-year-old with pink hockey socks could manage.

Georgia was a left winger, and as everyone else was always telling her, very small for her age. She never let that stop her, though. Out on the ice she was a force to be reckoned with. She was the type to wear her scrapes and bruises proudly, sometimes even adding glitter to them. She played on her team's top line with her best friends Millie and Lola, who played center and right wing respectively. Georgia knew her linemates had better shots than her, but she was the fastest (and had the fastest hands and feet, in her opinion).

Behind her were all the founding members of the Hurricanes, minus Millie, obviously. This included twins Ashlyn and Daylyn, who were the best defensive pair anyone could ever ask for, Khloe, their kooky goalie extraordinaire, and two more talented forwards named Sage and Violet.

The team was bigger than just the eight of them, of course; they had a completely full roster this year, but some of the girls were in grade three and some were from neighboring towns. Sadly, this meant they didn't get to experience the joy of skating on the pond after school during the winter as often.

Cameron didn't sympathize. He was still mad about his team being cut in half when the girls had just suddenly decided to leave them behind. See, a lot of people thought that girls weren't interested in hockey, but this was actually not the case at all, especially in this part of the state. There were a ton of girls who wanted to play, and so few teams that catered exclusively to them. So much so, that almost as soon as the Hurricanes put out the open call, every co-ed team in a twenty-mile radius suddenly lost all of its girls. They were able to create three teams in Novice, Atom, and Peewee, and were still growing.

Cameron was jealous, to be quite honest. The girls who used to be his friends and look up to him as their captain had completely left him in the dust, and they seemed to be having more fun by themselves than they ever had with him. Millie was even beating him in points this year, which he absolutely couldn't stand. The Lightning's goalie, Logan, who also happened to be Millie's cousin, was constantly telling Cameron that he was still the best player overall and should stop letting the numbers get to him, but that was easier said than done.

Luke, Cameron's hugely intimidating right-hand man, had apparently had enough of the girls' idle threats. He stepped out from behind Cameron and bent down to Georgia's level.

"You know the rules, pipsqueak," he said good-naturedly. "No captain, no pond."

"Yeah," Hunter echoed. "Not our fault that one of your players wasn't prepared."

Cameron could see the fight leaving Georgia and the rest of the girls. They'd already been waiting awhile, and they could only stall for so much longer. Another minute or so and the ice would belong to the Lightning. Part of him was disappointed that he wouldn't get to rub the victory in Millie's face.

But, naturally, they had spoken too soon.

Millie chose that exact moment to come barreling through the line of trees with her gear bag banging at her side and her stick held over her head as she ran.

"I'm...here!" she wheezed in between steps. "I'm here!"

Cameron shook his head and put his face in his hands.

"I gotta stop jinxing myself," he said under his breath.

Millie swapped her street shoes for skates and the rest of her equipment in record time and joined the standoff at center ice. She and Cameron faced off, staring daggers at each other.

It was just your typical, average Monday, really.

# 2

"WHAT THE HECK do you think you're doing?" Millie asked.

Cameron narrowed his eyes.

"Why, if it isn't Willy Millie herself," he drawled, using a nickname he knew she hated. "How nice of you to show up. I was just about to lead my much better team onto the ice, seeing as they were all here on time." His mouth twitched upward and his face was dripping with mock sympathy. "It's only fair. You wouldn't want old Mrs. Jefferson to hear that you girls weren't being fair with her precious little pond now, would you?"

Millie rolled her eyes.

"Cameron," she said. "I mean this in the meanest possible way: Go jump into a lake. Preferably one that's not frozen."

Cameron only shook his head and laughed at her. "I don't know why I'm surprised. It's not like I should expect you to be a good captain."

"Millie's a great captain!" Georgia shouted.

"Yeah," Ashlyn agreed. "You're just jealous cuz we like her better than you."

The comment hit way too close to home, but Cameron would never let them see that.

"The boys like me just fine," he said. "And besides, being a good captain isn't about being popular. It's about being reliable...like being on time, for instance."

Hunter and Luke fist bumped on either side of him. They were his wingmen, both on and off the ice. It was actually surprising that they worked so well together, considering how different they were. Luke was as laid-back as they came, while Hunter was the world's greatest overachiever, always looking to be the best at everything. Either way, they were both great hockey players and completely loyal to their team. To Cameron, that was all that really mattered.

"Well, thanks for the advice," said Millie, trying not to let her irritation show. "But I'm here now. And it's our day to have the ice, so if you could please just go away..." She made a shooing gesture with her hands.

Several of the Lightning boys laughed at her.

"Oh, Millie. Nice try, but you're just not very intimidating," Cameron said. "But don't feel bad. You'll probably be better when you're older."

Millie's eyes narrowed to slits.

"We're the same age, Cameron."

"My mom says that girls mature faster than boys," Logan chimed in.

Ben gave him a light smack on the back of the head, and Cameron turned back to glare at his goalie.

"Dude, whose side are you on?"

"Sorry," Logan said, hanging his head.

"Anyway," Cameron continued. "We're not leaving. We were here first. And *all* of us were here, mind you."

"That is such garbage, Cameron," said Daylyn, who was the biggest and toughest girl on the team. "Mondays are officially ours. Khloe signed us up for this time slot like three weeks ago. Right, Khloe?"

Khloe shrank back and hid her face in her gloves. She looked like a turtle disappearing into its shell.

"I uh, I know I said I would, but it, um...it might have slipped my mind..."

"KHLOE!" the girls all shouted in unison.

"I know! I'm sorry," she said, popping out from behind her gloves. "I'm a failure to goalies everywhere!"

Khloe was always saying weird things like that. There was this stereotype within the hockey community about goalies always being a little bit strange, but Khloe took that to an entirely new level. Then again, Logan wasn't anything like that, and neither was Khloe's older brother who was also a goalie, so maybe she was just a bit quirky.

Millie's shoulders slumped in defeat. They

had been through this dozens of times before and she knew they were never going to reach a compromise. They'd just stand here arguing until it got dark or somebody gave up. That somebody definitely wasn't going to be her, and it probably wasn't going to be Cameron either, which meant nobody was getting the ice. Not tonight. What a shame.

"Why don't you all just play together?" suggested a sweet fourth grader who was watching them from the sidelines.

"No!" they all shouted back.

At least the two teams could agree on something.

A whistle sounded in the distance, and the kids looked up just in time to see Jon and Bev emerge from behind the trees. Jon and Bev were five years older than the rest of the kids. Back when the girls and boys were all playing on the Lightning together, the pair would often catch the younger kids on their way in and out of the rec center and stop to give them helpful tips for improving their game. The two of them didn't play competitive hockey now that they were in high school, but they still watched every Lightning and Hurricanes home game and often acted as referees/peacekeepers down at the pond.

"What are you guys fighting about now?" Jon asked, coming to join them at center ice.

Millie and Cameron looked down at their feet, too embarrassed to admit their pettiness to Jon, whom they both really admired.

"We're arguing about who gets the pond today," Logan admitted.

Jon sighed. "Of course you are."

Bev smiled kindly. She secretly thought the whole rivalry was kind of cute.

"Didn't we settle this last time?" she asked.

"Well I *thought* we did," Millie said, with a pointed look over at Cameron.

Cameron shrugged.

"I just came to see if the ice was taken, and it wasn't. The girls were all just standing around waiting for you. How is that fair?"

"Oh, I'll show you fair," Millie said, taking a step forward. Jon blocked her progress with his arm.

"None of that, please," he said. "I think it's time we settled this. Once and for all, right Bev?"

Bev let loose a devious smile. "What did you have in mind?"

Jon leaned over to whisper something in her ear and her eyes lit up. She nodded enthusiastically and then took a moment to collect herself before announcing the plan to the rest of the group.

"Friday night we will have a game," she said slowly, being overly dramatic. "Girls versus boys. Hurricanes versus Lightning. Whoever wins gets the ice right after school every day for the rest of the season."

The kids stared at each other and then back at Bev. There was a competitive twinkle in all of their eyes.

"Sound fair?" Jon asked.

Cameron and Millie gathered both teams for a quick huddle.

"We're in," said Cameron after a moment.

"Us too," Millie agreed.

"Then it's settled," Bev said. "You guys can take turns practicing. Girls take today and Wednesday, and boys get Tuesday and Thursday."

Millie gave Cameron one final challenging look.

"It is so on."

# 3

***Two Years Earlier***

"LET'S GO, CAM!" Millie shouted from her spot on the bench.

She hated not being out on the ice with him anymore, but there was one advantage to being on separate lines. It meant that they always got to cheer each other on.

To her left was Lola, who was resting her head on Millie's shoulder after a really long shift.

"You two should just get married already," she wheezed. She sounded like Millie's grandpa did after he'd spent a few minutes chasing her around the front yard.

Millie rolled her eyes. "Gross. He's my best friend."

Millie and Cameron were like family, like twins who had been born to different moms. They did everything together. Hockey, video games, movies. Even the boring stuff like schoolwork.

Millie admired Cameron more than anyone else in the whole world. More than Sidney Crosby, even! If she was being honest with herself, she was also a bit jealous of his natural talent. Millie felt like she had to work twice as hard to master skills that came so easily to him. Not to mention that Cameron was a great leader. Even though he was the best player on the Lightning, maybe even in their whole league, he was never mean about it. He was great at making sure that everyone on his team felt appreciated and that they all got a chance to shine.

Millie wasn't like that at all. She saw each game as a chance to show off everything she had been practicing, even plays that were a little risky. A lot of the time it cost her team goals, but Millie couldn't help it. She just wanted to prove herself and maybe, one day, be half the captain that Cameron was.

Millie looked back down at the ice where Cameron was chasing the puck. She cheered for him again, this time a bit self-consciously.

She knew that a lot of people didn't understand their friendship or why the two of them were so close—and to be honest, she didn't really understand it herself sometimes. It had just always been this way. Millie and Cameron against everyone else.

Sure, Lola and Georgia were amazing. So were Sage and Violet and all of the boys. She loved them. How could she not? They'd all been playing together for as long as she could remember. They had history, as her mom would say.

But with Cameron it was different. Even if the world turned upside down and hockey suddenly stopped existing (even though that'd be super sucky and terrible), she knew that Cameron would always have her back.

Wasn't that what best friends were for?

There were three important things in Cameron's life: hockey, his family, and Millie. And those three things were all tangled together like a fancy knot. He started playing hockey because his family loved it. He loved playing hockey because he got to do it with Millie. And he loved Millie because she was practically family.

Cameron had known Millie since the day he was born. She was exactly three weeks older. In fact, resting on his mantel back home was a picture of Millie's mom holding Cameron and Cameron's mom holding Millie in the hospital room when he was just a few hours old. In the picture, both moms were smiling wide and looking down at each other's babies, as if already knowing they would be best friends for life, just like their parents were.

So Millie and Cameron had learned to crawl and walk and speak together. They spent tons of hours camped out in each other's living rooms making up silly games and building forts out of couch cushions. When Millie cried,

Cameron cried. When Cameron cried, Millie hugged him and told him that everything was going to be okay, that she was there for him. That she'd always be there.

But some things were just too good to be true.

These days she was spending less and less time with him. Saying things like, Lola and I are going to try on dresses for her aunt's wedding! or, Georgia and I are having a sleepover, girls only, sorry!

Cameron missed the days when they were learning how to skate, hands held out for balance and their feet shuffling forward, until eventually, skating felt as natural as walking. Then it became more like flying, especially on the rec center's perfect and glossy ice. Playing with Millie these last couple of years had been the coolest thing that ever happened to him. They were a perfect pair, like Batman and Robin.

At least, they had been until Millie decided she wanted to play center, just like him. That was the thing about Millie. Once she got her heart set on something, there was no stopping her. Everyone else was just along for the ride.

He just hoped that wherever she was going, there was room for him, too.

Out of all the kids on the Lightning's roster, nobody understood how the team worked quite like Logan. It was a perk of being a goalie. You got to stay out on the ice for the whole game and watch the action from a place that nobody else got to see it from.

Logan was like that off the ice too. Quiet. Observant. Always lurking in the background and trying his best to keep the peace—he hated it when his friends fought.

Logan was the first to notice everything. He noticed when everyone started slowly growing taller than Georgia. He picked up on the fact that Linkin had a secret crush on Violet. He knew that Rhys only liked grossing out the girls because he felt threatened by them, and he figured out that Preston was super rich months before he invited them all to his family's mansion for his seventh birthday.

Also, even though everyone would laugh and

call him crazy if they knew, he could see that his cousin and Cameron were slowly starting to drift away from each other, like pool floaties without someone's arms stuck in them.

The worst part was that there was nothing he could do about it. Especially since nobody could see it but him. It was like one of those times where he saw the puck coming at him, but he just couldn't make the save no matter how hard he tried.

So Logan did what he was great at: He crossed his fingers and waited to see what would happen.

# 4

AS SOON AS the boys left the ice, the Hurricanes got to work.

"There is no way we're losing that game," Millie said, and she meant it.

She knew that her team had the Lightning beat in the skills department, but that didn't mean much if they couldn't get past Linkin and Ben, both of whom seemed to be growing more and more massive each day. To combat this, she set up a special drill. While most of the team was having a 3-on-3 scrimmage at center ice, the extra player would drag Khloe (who was lying on her stomach) around the perimeter of the pond by her stick. These pull drills were killer on the legs and arms, but they were the best way Millie knew to build up enough strength to push past people who were twice, or even triple, their size. Each girl, except Khloe of course, had a turn.

Then they moved on to a quick relay, which involved jumping over three sticks, swerving around one of the team's two defenders, and taking a shot on Khloe. Millie's time was the fastest, but Georgia also did particularly well, as she always did with timed challenges. Lola had a bit of a rough time making it past Daylyn, but once she finally did, her shot was the first and only one to make it past a squared-up and determined Khloe. Violet and Sage managed to get around the defenders pretty easily. So basically, the relay was a great way to challenge everyone all at once.

Next came the shootout, which was everyone's favorite drill. They all got one chance to start at center ice, carry the puck and shoot it in whatever manner they pleased. It was a great way to get creative and practice those flashy trick shots that they saw on TV, but were rarely allowed to try at the rec center. Khloe was so determined and unfazed on the ice that it made coming up with new ways to get by her even more fun.

After that, Millie had them skate around freely and work on individual puck handling. Millie herself was getting a bit too aggressive with it, tossing her puck so high in the air that it was more likely to smack her in the face than land neatly on her stick. She was throwing all of her frustrations about Cameron into practicing, and by the time the sun was dipping lower in the sky she had to be practically dragged off of the ice.

Back at her house, the eight of them sat cross-legged before the crackling fire drinking hot chocolate, eating pizza, and discussing strategy.

Or at least, *Millie* was trying to discuss strategy. Everyone else seemed more interested in gossiping.

"Lighten up, Mills," Georgia said, plopping down next to her with a slice of cheese pizza folded up slightly in her hand. "We can beat the boys. It's not like we haven't done it before."

Millie didn't want to be the one to point out that every time they'd beaten the boys, it had been with a full team, and not just the eight of them. Instead, she sighed, doing her best to turn off her hockey brain and enjoy this unplanned bit of fun with her friends.

Khloe was sitting with a whole box of pepperoni and mushroom pizza on her lap. Khloe's heart was definitely located in her stomach. That girl would eat everything in sight if she could. It was hard to tell sometimes whether she liked food or hockey more. Lucky for her, Sage was on a baking kick lately, which meant that she got to be the official taste tester. For Khloe, that was a dream come true.

Ashlyn and Daylyn were hunched over together in the corner of the room looking at funny videos on Millie's mom's iPad. You'd think it would be easy to forget they were twins with how different they acted—Ash was smart and bookish, intensely into strategic defense, while Day was big and tough and just wanted to beat up on all the boys—but the way they moved around each other on the ice and stuck together off of it was a dead giveaway. They had Millie convinced that twin telepathy actually existed.

Lola was lying on her stomach and lazily drawing in her sketchbook while telling a joke to Violet, who was listening intently and grinning nonstop. That was the two of their personalities in a nutshell. Lola was hilarious, but too shy to just be herself without distracting her nervous hands and brain with drawing. She was actually pretty good at it too, one of the most talented artists in their grade. Violet, on the other hand, didn't have any particular hobbies or interests outside of hockey. She was just really kind and really attentive to everyone she met. She was a great listener and gave really good advice (and hugs for that matter).

Then of course there was Georgia, competitive and feisty, but intensely loyal. Lover of all things girly, but never letting that stop her from playing hockey, or doing any of the other things she enjoyed.

Millie loved them all so much. She wanted them to keep playing together for as long as possible. Even though she had no plans to retire from hockey in high school like Jon and Bev had (Millie had her sights set on the big leagues), she knew that some of her friends might. If that was the case, she only had a limited amount of time to make them the best they could be.

And she would, right after this next slice of pizza.

# 5

AS HE LED his team off the ice and through the park, Cameron felt important and dignified. Or at least, he did until everyone started busting up laughing behind him.

Cameron's eye twitched. He turned around slowly to find the rest of his crew circled around Rhys, who had his mouth open wide with his tongue out, about to put it on the flag pole. Cameron marched up to him and smacked him lightly on the back of the head.

"Dude. That's not funny. The last thing we need is you getting your tongue stuck on that pole when we've got a competition to win."

Rhys swallowed slightly and gave Cameron a sheepish grin. Cameron just shook his head and walked away. Times like these were when he missed Millie the most. She had a way of bossing people around without sounding like a nagging babysitter. It was a skill Cameron was quite jealous of, not that he'd ever tell her that.

The eight of them managed to walk the rest of the short distance to Cameron's house without any further shenanigans. In the living room, Cameron's mom was lying with her feet propped up on the couch. There was a box of cookies resting on her stomach as she watched a home renovation show. She glanced over at the door as the children walked in. Her eyes briefly met Cameron's before landing on his brood of unannounced guests. Cameron could practically feel her internal sigh, but she didn't complain. She just got up and walked to the kitchen to start scraping together enough food for everybody. Cameron made a mental note to go all out on this year's Mother's Day gift.

After that, the Lightning boys were banished to the basement with chips, soda, and sandwiches. Lucky for Cameron, he had the coolest basement in the whole wide world.

There was a foosball table and an ancient air hockey machine, not to mention a pool table for the grown-ups. There was also an entire closet full of board games and a soft fluffy rug splayed out in front of a giant TV with multiple gaming consoles.

Cameron flopped down in his bean bag and turned on the most recent NHL game. Then he scanned the room. He only had four controllers, and he had to be strategic about who he gave the other three to if he wanted to keep his high score.

Certainly not Rhys, he thought. The boy was laughing and shoving food in his face, never one for taking things seriously. Sometimes Cameron enjoyed his friend's silly antics, but today wasn't one of those days.

Then there were Ben and Preston, who didn't much care for video games. Ben was more into comics and more old-fashioned nerdy things, while Preston had just never developed a taste for them. Anytime you gave him a controller he would just scowl at it and press random buttons for a few minutes before passing it on to someone else.

Linkin, he was a great guy and all, but video

games were definitely not his forte. He was an amazing defenseman, and super loyal, but he also needed a lot of guidance, both in video games and on the ice. Logan had the opposite problem. He had skills, but he was too quiet and usually kept what he was doing to himself until it was too late.

Hunter was not someone he wanted to play against. He was incredibly good at this game, but also super competitive, and if things didn't go his way, he'd pout about it for the rest of the night. Luke had the opposite problem. He didn't care whether he won or lost, at least as far as video games were concerned.

Cameron chewed on his lip and finally handed them over to Luke, Logan, and Linkin. The three L's. There had to be some sort of luckiness in that, right?

As the four of them got to playing, Cameron leaned back and casually posed the question: "So how are we gonna beat the girls?"

For a moment there was silence, followed by laughter.

"As if they would ever be a threat to us," Hunter said.

Preston and Rhys whooped in agreement. Cameron paused the game and snuck a glance over at his co-players. Luke shrugged as if he didn't have an opinion one way or the other, and Linkin was still staring intently at the screen as if he hadn't yet realized the game was on pause. Logan kept quiet, as usual.

Cameron sighed and turned to face his group.

"Look guys. This is serious. Whether you want to believe it or not, the girls are good. If there are any weak links among us, they will sniff it out and use it against us. If we want to keep the pond for the rest of the year, we need to be at the top of our game."

"Cameron's right," Ben spoke up. "Remember the skills comp? Our teams were pretty much equal. Plus the Hurricanes have the better record so far this year."

"Violet always pushes right past me," Linkin said almost wistfully.

"Khloe's a monster in goal," Logan agreed.

"And Millie's unpredictable," said Cameron. "So we need to be too."

Nobody objected, so Cameron cracked his knuckles, unpaused his game, and started talking strategy.

# 6

ON TUESDAY MORNING the halls of Dakota Elementary School seemed more crowded than usual. Instead of milling about freely, clusters of students lined the halls, eyes darting wildly and their heads on a swivel. There was anxious whispering from every corner, and the upcoming matchup seemed to be the topic of every conversation—conversations that seemed to stop abruptly any time one of the Lightning boys or Hurricane girls came into view.

On top of this tension, Millie and Cameron were slinging insults at each other as if they got paid to do it. Same as always. The rest of the student body fell into their predictable sides, with most of the girls backing Millie and most of the boys backing Cameron, just for appearances' sake.

But although the two captains were the loudest, they certainly did not speak for everyone on their teams. If you were paying close enough attention, you might have noticed Ben and Lola secretly meeting up in the band room between classes to share drawings.

"I call this one Captain Cockatiel," Ben said, holding up a colorful picture of a bird with an eyepatch and a sword slung over its back. He was flying through the air like a superhero.

Lola giggled and held up a half finished sketch of Ben she'd been working on for days. Ben's face lit up with glee as he admired the detail.

"Can you teach me how to shade like that?" he asked.

Lola bit her lip and glanced out the window to make sure nobody was looking at them before nodding.

Meanwhile, at the other end of the school,

Linkin was busy stuffing a sappy love note into Violet's desk while she and her friends were out at recess. They'd been writing notes back and forth for almost a year now. Linkin thought she was pretty, and smart, and super awesome to talk to. He couldn't tell the others about it, though. He was pretty certain Cameron would yell at him for "fraternizing with the enemy." Whatever that meant.

Of course, he wasn't the only one fraternizing.

During lunch, while Sage was handing out her most recent batch of cookies, she slyly handed one off to Preston as he was walking by. The two of them didn't even look at each other or acknowledge the exchange, but Preston appreciated the gesture nonetheless.

In art class, when Mrs. Phillips asked them to get their supplies from their cubbies, Luke automatically grabbed Georgia's at the same time as his, without even thinking about it. He knew she couldn't reach it on her own and hated asking for help, so it had just become a habit at this point.

In math, when Rhys slammed his textbook

down on the desk and hung his head in confusion, Ashlyn slid her chair up and did her best to explain how to divide fractions. She used a hockey metaphor, of course. She could tell Rhys understood it by the way his eyebrows unfurrowed and he let out his usual carefree grin.

Constantly overachieving Hunter was having an off day in gym. He kept getting hit in the face by dodgeballs and stalling the whole game for everyone. When some of the other kids started laughing at his misfortune and calling him names, Daylyn stepped in and chewed them out. Her words were so vicious that Coach Vasquez threatened to send her to the office. It was worth it, though. If anyone was going to make fun of that loser, it was going to be her.

Finally, at the end of the day when Khloe lost track of time and missed her bus, Logan jogged over to her and offered to walk her home so she wouldn't be lonely. The two of them hobbled along side by side, weighed down by backpacks that were almost as big as they were. It was no problem, though. Goalies were used to carrying a lot of weight on their shoulders.

All of these gestures taken at face value were small and easy to ignore, but the message behind them was clear: The ties between the Lightning and the Hurricanes were not as broken as everyone seemed to think.

# 7

LATER THAT AFTERNOON, the Lightning boys were taking full advantage of their day with the pond to work on problem areas and practice their most successful plays.

"Bend your knees more," Cameron told Ben.

Ben nodded and skated away with his large legs slightly bent, just as instructed.

Being back on the ice had settled something in Cameron, making him calmer and more confident than he had been in a while. Here, he was in his element. He could see everyone's weaknesses so clearly: *Adjust your grip. Shoot from farther away. Eyes on your own man.*

They were all tiny things, easily fixable, but

Cameron couldn't help but notice them. And it was that attention to detail that was going to help them beat the girls, once and for all.

After just a few practice scrimmages, they were working like a well-oiled machine. So much so, that Cameron decided to ditch his drill sergeant attitude and have a little fun. He handed out individual pucks and had everyone line up and shoot all at once, sending a massive stream of pucks Logan's way. Logan handled the barrage as well as could be expected, gliding from one end of his crease to the other and scooping up as many pucks as he could and throwing them back.

As the pucks came back at them, the boys took it upon themselves to attempt the wildest and most ridiculous trick shots they could imagine. Several boys spun around laughing and kicked the puck in (which was totally illegal, but it looked cool). Hunter served his puck up in the air and batted it in with his stick. He looked mildly devastated when Logan easily knocked the shot away.

Cameron took a more realistic approach.

He aimed for the crossbar and watched with bated breath as it bounced off and into the net just above Logan's left shoulder.

He smiled widely as everyone circled around him and clapped him on the back. He found that he was no longer worried about what was going to happen on Friday. In fact, he was actually looking forward to it. Right then, Cameron felt like he could take on the whole world.

Meanwhile, on the other side of town, the girls were perched in front of Khloe's dad's giant flatscreen. They were watching footage of the boys' last couple of games, which Khloe's older brother who worked at the rec center had generously "borrowed" for them.

Millie was shoving popcorn into her mouth without taking her eyes off the screen. She was completely entranced by the game, just like she was when she was watching the pros. Even though she knew that she shouldn't be, she couldn't help the little pang of pride she felt when the Lightning beat their competition, winning the game 3-1.

"They've gotten a lot better since last time we played them," Ashlyn said, sounding worried.

Millie hummed and picked up the remote. She rewound to the opposing team's one and only goal. It had been a completely accidental tap-in. No skill involved whatsoever.

"They're good," Millie agreed. "But we have something they don't."

She let the pause drag on for dramatic effect.

"And what would that be?" Georgia asked finally, cutting through the silence.

Millie grinned.

"The element of surprise."

The rest of the girls looked at her skeptically as if she'd just lost every single one of her marbles.

"Think about it," Millie explained, standing up on her chair. "Out of all the games we've watched today, how many risks did you see the Lightning take?"

"Zero," said Sage.

"Negative 42," Lola echoed under her breath.

"Exactly," Millie said, hands on her hips. "To beat them we've just gotta play smart and strong like we always do, and throw in a little bit of extra bravery."

"I'm down for being brave," Khloe said, flopping her legs over the side of her armchair. "Although I don't really have a choice. I'll have pucks flying at my face."

Georgia patted their goalie's arm and said, "Millie's right. If we spice things up, the boys won't know what hit 'em."

Millie smiled and hopped down from her chair.

"Hurricanes on three?" she suggested, holding out her hand.

The rest of the team quickly followed suit. Their chant was so loud that it shook the windows and made Khloe's mom yell at them to be quiet.

# 8

VIOLET WAS NERVOUS all Wednesday morning. When she'd gotten to school, there was a note in her desk from Linkin asking her to meet him behind the gym during recess. Sure, they talked and hung out all the time, but he'd never asked her to meet up at school before. School was a neutral zone. No contact whatsoever. She had no idea what could be important enough to break this rule. She just hoped everything was okay.

When the time came, she easily snuck away from her friends by saying that she had to check in with Mr. Greenfield about a missing homework assignment. She fed the same lie to the teacher on playground duty and headed back toward the main building, turning and making a beeline for the gym as soon as she was certain that nobody was looking. She knew nobody would suspect her of anything. She didn't get in trouble. She got people *out* of trouble. It was kind of her thing.

Once she reached the shaded awning outside the gym, she stopped to catch her breath. Then, pausing to wipe her sweaty palms on her jeans, she walked around to the back of the building to meet Linkin.

Linkin was wearing his usual black pants and red flannel shirt, buttoned all the way to his neck. Overtop of the whole thing was a puffy yellow jacket that clashed with just about everything, but that was part of its charm. He was pacing back and forth, hands in his pockets and new sneakers squeaking against the slippery sidewalk.

"Hey," Violet said softly, stopping him mid-step.

Linkin turned around so quickly he almost fell down.

"Hey," he breathed, looking at her the same

way someone might look at a deer they were trying not to spook.

"What's up?" Violet asked, moving closer. She thought Linkin was cute when he was all nervous and awkward.

Linkin hung his head and nodded, almost as if he was trying to psych himself up for something.

"I don't think we should hang out anymore," Linkin said.

Violet must have looked as troubled as she felt because Linkin quickly added, "At least, not until after the game."

"Where's this coming from?" Violet asked, leading him to the brick wall, where they sat down with their backs against the building.

Linkin sighed.

"I just feel bad going behind Cameron's back. I'm worried he's gonna find out and yell at me. He's been super on edge lately. This stuff with Millie is really getting to him."

"It's getting to all of us," Violet agreed. "But that doesn't mean we have to let it decide who we hang out with. We're not doing anything wrong. Besides, my mom already said she'd take us to see that new detective movie after school tomorrow."

"The animated one?"

"Yep."

Linkin squished his eyebrows together.

"Well, in that case, I *suppose* I could swing by your house after practice tomorrow..."

Violet laughed and reached out to squeeze Linkin's hand, causing his entire face to turn red. She opened her mouth to tell him it was a plan, but was interrupted by a loud coughing noise to her left.

Violet let go of Linkin's hand and glanced up to see Mr. Greenfield looming over them with his eyes narrowed and hands on his hips. He looked slowly from one kid to the other with a scowl on his face.

"Hey, Violet. So what's this I hear about a missing homework assignment?"

Violet's stomach sank. It seemed like her record for not getting into trouble had just been broken.

# 9

UPON RETURNING TO class after recess, Millie couldn't help but notice the empty seat toward the back of the room which usually belonged to Violet. Her absence was incredibly odd. Violet was not one for skipping class or leaving early. Not to mention she'd been acting weird all day.

Millie leaned over to get Kendra Mitchell's attention.

"Hey, do you know what happened to Violet?" Millie whispered.

Kendra's eyes went wide as saucers and she nodded her head enthusiastically. Kendra was just opening her mouth to speak when Mrs. Smith glanced over at her in warning. The two of them went back to silently reading, properly chastised. Millie was so curious that she didn't absorb a single word of the text.

After a few moments had gone by, she felt a light tap on her shoulder. Millie looked up at Kendra and quickly snatched the folded-up note dangling from the other girl's fingertips before Mrs. Smith could see.

The note read:

Susan B. swears she saw Violet getting dragged into the principal's office with Linkin Marsh.

Millie held up her book in front of her face and wrote underneath Kendra's words in thick black ink.

## What 4?

She slid the note back and watched Kendra out of the corner of her eye. It seemed like she was writing forever. When she finally handed the paper back it said:

IDK. Fighting probably. What else could it be? Those two hate each other. All of u hockey kids do.

Millie chewed her bottom lip and stuffed the note into her back pocket without further comment. Truthfully, she couldn't think of any other reason they'd be sent to the office together either, but she also couldn't picture Violet fighting with anyone, even one of the Lightning boys. She usually left that to Millie, Georgia, and Daylyn. They were the scrappy ones on the team.

And Linkin...sure, he was big and capable of doing some serious damage, but he wasn't mean or dangerous (at least, not off the ice). Millie had a hard time believing he would react violently toward anyone. Especially a sweet, practical girl who was half his size.

Then again, Cameron did have his hooks in him pretty tightly...

Millie shook her head. She needed to stop. If she kept going around in circles like this she was going to drive herself crazy. The only way to get answers was to be patient and wait for Violet to return.

Only Violet didn't return.

The bell rang, signaling the end of the school day, and the forward was still nowhere to be found.

Millie frowned and packed up her things before heading out into the hallway. She made an immediate beeline for the drinking fountain where Georgia and Lola were already waiting for her.

"Did you hear about Vi?" Millie asked before she even came to a full stop.

Both girls shook their heads.

"No," said Georgia. "What's up?"

Millie leaned down and took a sip of water from the fountain before popping back up and giving them the scoop.

"Someone told me she and Linkin got sent home for fighting," she said. "That's ridiculous, right?"

Georgia agreed right away, but Lola wasn't so convinced. She was looking around and biting her lip nervously.

"I don't know," she began. "Linkin's in my class and he was missing all afternoon too..."

"What could Linkin have possibly said to set her off that badly?" Georgia asked. "Violet's like a wise old mentor. She's our *Dumbledore!* Dumbledore doesn't get sent to the principal's office for fighting."

"That's because Dumbledore *is* the principal," Lola said under her breath.

Millie rolled her eyes at both of them.

"If not fighting, I don't know what else it could be," she said.

The three of them stood in silence for a couple of seconds, trying (and failing) to figure it all out.

Millie caught sight of Cameron moving toward them on his way to the main exit. He

was alone and seemed to be walking faster than normal. The two captains locked eyes. Cameron looked away quickly, but not quickly enough to hide his worry. Millie could sense that he'd heard about the incident and was just as confused by it as she was.

She couldn't let it show, though. That's not what a good captain would do. Good captains didn't dwell on things that were out of their control.

"There's no use trying to figure it out now," Millie said. "Go home and get suited up. It's our last day with the pond before the game on Friday and we need to make the most of it. Who knows? Maybe Violet will show up at practice and explain how this was all just some big misunderstanding."

Lola and Georgia looked doubtful, but they did as she asked and went their separate ways.

Later at the pond, Millie led practice, down by one player. It was difficult, and all of their scrimmages were uneven and off-balance, but as her Nana said, the show must go on.

Deep down beneath her calm appearance,

though, Millie was really starting to freak out. Fighting would get them both grounded and who knew for how long. At this point, she wasn't even sure Linkin and Violet would be allowed to play on Friday at all.

# 10

THURSDAY WAS NOT being kind to Linkin.

First, he'd slept through his alarm, missing the bus by at least an hour. Then he had to wake up his mom—who had worked all night and was still mad at him for getting in trouble at school—and ask for a ride. Then, he had to sit and wait for the office lady to write him a late pass. And *then* he had to enter his class-room where everyone kept giving him sly looks that weren't really sly at all.

Thankfully, his teacher, Mr. Cortez, was a real no-nonsense type, meaning nobody disrupted class to address the elephant in the room.

That brief string of luck couldn't last, though.

They had to break for electives at eleven. Each class in their grade alternated between art, music, gym, and library time. Today, Linkin's class had music. It was usually really fun: They all gathered in a circle on the band room floor and blew into their colorful plastic recorders or pressed down on ancient keyboards with the notes Sharpie-d onto the keys.

Linkin spent the entire hour blowing into somebody else's bassoon to avoid talking to people. It actually worked surprisingly well. Bassoons are just naturally repulsive. He just hoped that this kid had cleaned his spit valve recently—if bassoons even had spit valves, that is.

After music came lunch, and this was where it became *really* impossible to avoid his teammates. Specifically, his nosy captain.

"Okay," Cameron said, blocking Linkin's way out of the cafeteria. "Time to spill. What happened between you and Violet?"

Linkin's shoulders scrunched up so high that he looked like a sad turtle.

"I don't wanna talk about it," he said,

pushing his way past Cameron with brute strength alone.

Cameron quickly caught up to him and trailed after him in the busy hallway.

"Come on, man! You've been acting weird about it all day. Just tell me what happened. Whatever it is, I've got your back."

Linkin highly doubted that.

"I said I don't want to talk about it, Cam," Linkin yelled, causing some nervous younger kids to glance their way.

At that, Cameron finally stormed off in a huff and left him alone. Alas, Cameron wasn't the only person who wanted answers. Linkin felt like he was dodging his teammates left and right. Ben was in his class and constantly staring at him like a puzzle he couldn't figure out. Logan tried to corner him at recess for hot gossip. Not to mention, any time he passed by one of the girls in the hall, they gave him the stink eye.

It was all too much.

Linkin was terrible at this. And he felt terrible too. It figured that the one and only time he asked to see Violet at school would be the time they got caught. He was actually somewhat relieved that they'd been caught by a teacher and not a student. That meant they could still keep their secret, but at the same time, having everyone think that he'd actually *hurt* Violet in some way made his stomach ache.

In many ways, Mr. Greenfield had completely overreacted. He'd given them one detention each, called their parents, and given them direct orders to "avoid public displays of affection" at school. It was ridiculous. They were just holding hands, not plotting world domination. If he wasn't so afraid of everyone finding out that he liked Violet, maybe he'd stage a protest. The news would probably love that. He could see the headlines now: *"Young Boy Fights For Love And Justice!"* People would eat that right up.

Or maybe they'd just laugh at him. Linkin wouldn't be surprised. Right then, he felt like the world's biggest screwup. He could never do anything right. He just wanted to get through the rest of the school day and that afternoon's practice as quickly as possible, so he could go home and be miserable in peace.

Violet felt just as bad, if not worse. As far as she was concerned, it had been her fault they'd gotten in trouble. She was the one who had decided to hold Linkin's hand. If she hadn't done that, maybe Mr. Greenfield would have just yelled at them to get back to the playground and left it at that.

She didn't know what she'd been thinking, sneaking away like that in the first place. It wasn't like her, even though she wanted it to be. She wanted to be the kind of person who leapt into things without fear, the way some of her tougher friends did. She wanted to be the kind of girl who stood up for her friends and would do anything to make them smile, but the truth was, she was nervous and scared and she hated getting in trouble. She had never had detention in her life! And as much as Daylyn assured her it was "no big deal," she didn't want to make a pattern of it either.

What she wanted more than anything was to

talk about all of this with someone, someone who knew the whole story and wouldn't make her feel weird about it. Someone who would tell her that it wasn't her fault and that Mr. Greenfield was lame and wouldn't know fun if it smacked him in the side of the face like a dodgeball.

The only problem was, that person was Linkin: AKA, the one person she wasn't supposed to see. Literally any time they came anywhere near each other, there was a teammate or teacher there to steer them off in different directions.

For the first time in her life, Violet felt like she understood her older sister perfectly. If relationships were this hard at ten, she could only imagine what it must be like for teenagers. No wonder Shannon was so dramatic all the time. *Ugh.*

When the final bell rang and they were all dismissed for the afternoon, Violet lined up for the bus and rode home by herself, feeling defeated.

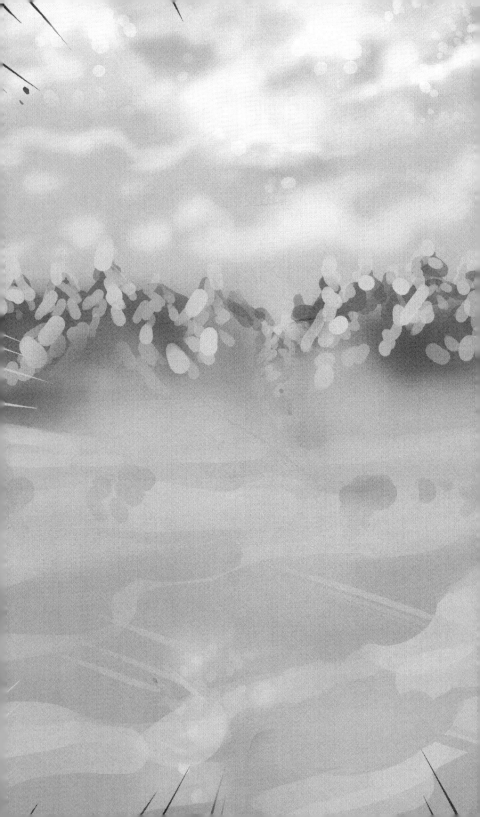

# 11

FRIDAY CAME FASTER than anyone could
have imagined, and the halls of Dakota Elementary School remained uncommonly quiet
as the kids slowly started filtering in. Nobody
was lingering by the bathrooms or the drinking
fountains to gossip and crack jokes. Nobody
was shouting or pitting one team against the
other. Everyone was just silently moving about
on the way to their classrooms like good little
children who could sense the tension in the air
and didn't want to get caught up in the drama.
Since the two teams were named after Lightning and Hurricanes, one might call this the
calm before the storm.

The eight Lightning boys arrived at school

separately like they always did, but today they met up in the quad exactly six minutes before the first bell so they could enter the building together as teammates. Much like their classmates, the boys were incredibly quiet. Half of them were wracked with nerves, and those nerves were contagious. It didn't help that their unified entrance made them the center of attention.

Most nervous of them all was Preston, though he'd never show it. He was obsessed with keeping his cool off the ice. And if *he* couldn't keep it together, how would any of the others? So he plastered on a fake smile and confidently stepped in front of Cameron to lead the pack, if only for a moment. He just hoped they couldn't tell how fast his heart was beating.

Meanwhile, the Hurricanes had taken more of a "divide and conquer" strategy for the beginning of the school day. Millie, Lola, and Georgia had carpooled, as had Ashlyn, Daylyn, and Sage; and Violet had volunteered to take the bus with Khloe. It was important that each girl was always with one of her teammates, otherwise their matching, handmade, sparkly pink T-shirts would be for nothing.

The shirts, naturally, had been Georgia's idea. She'd made each one with its wearer in mind. For instance, hers said *Hockey Princess*, while Khloe's said *Nothing Gets Past Me*, with a tiny picture of a goalpost. Daylyn's was a nice and simple *Lightning Sucks*, and her twin was sporting *Girls Run The World* with a tiny little globe at the bottom. Lola's said *Check Me Out* (she was particularly proud of that pun). *Stanley Cup-cakes* and *Hurricanes Rule* belonged to Sage and Violet respectively. Finally, there was Millie, whose shirt just said *World's Best Captain*.

The shirts seemed to be a big hit among their classmates, especially the other girls. Granted, they were all done in glitter glue and probably wouldn't survive their first run-in with the washing machine, but Georgia was proud of them nevertheless.

As the day went on, all of the fourth-grade teachers remained on edge, waiting for a fight to break out. Each of them had at least two of the pond kids in their care, and watching them stare meaningfully at each other all day was pretty darn stressful. Especially for old Mrs. Washington, who had not two, but five hockey players in her class: Ashlyn, Sage, Preston, Logan, and Rhys, all seated as far away from each other as possible.

They needn't have worried, though. The kids were all on their best behavior. They knew that even a little bit of trash talking could get their parents called and today's game canceled. Besides, they were more than willing to save all the nastiness for the ice. Even Rhys, AKA the world's biggest class clown, was managing to keep his mouth shut.

When electives came around, Luke held down Khloe's feet as she did pushups in the gym, and right across the hall were Linkin, Cameron, Ben, and Lola, painting their clay sculptures side by side. Daylyn and Hunter swapped books with each other in the library without saying a word.

At lunch, all sixteen of them sat at one long

table, boys on the left and girls on the right. There was something incredibly satisfying about staring your competition straight in the eye while chewing on rectangular pizza and fruit. Violet was the only one who didn't seem into it, lazily stirring her yogurt and refusing to look up and meet Linkin's eyes. She was too afraid of what she might see in them, since she still hadn't gotten the chance to apologize.

Recess wasn't much better. The two teams mostly kept to themselves except for Linkin, who snuck off to fill up his cup and nearly plowed headfirst into Georgia. From the out-side, it must have looked pretty funny, this giant dude bumping into this tiny girl, but it didn't feel funny. Linkin felt like he needed to apol-ogize, but he didn't know if it was a good idea to apologize to the enemy. Eventually Georgia just pushed right on past him and Linkin let her go.

The rest of the day passed incredibly slowly, and the more time passed, the more nervous the kids got. Some of them handled it well, by singing or cracking jokes, but others were

sweating and stammering and generally feeling like they were about to throw up.

And in the middle of it all were the two captains, Millie and Cameron. Neither of them heard a word of what their teachers had to say for the final twenty minutes of class. Millie was gripping her pencil too tightly and imagining scoring the winning goal later. Cameron was breathing deeply and bouncing his leg under his desk. Both of them were counting down the seconds until the game.

When the bell finally rang, they both stood up quickly and ran out the door without waiting to be dismissed. It was time for them to show each other what their teams were really made of.

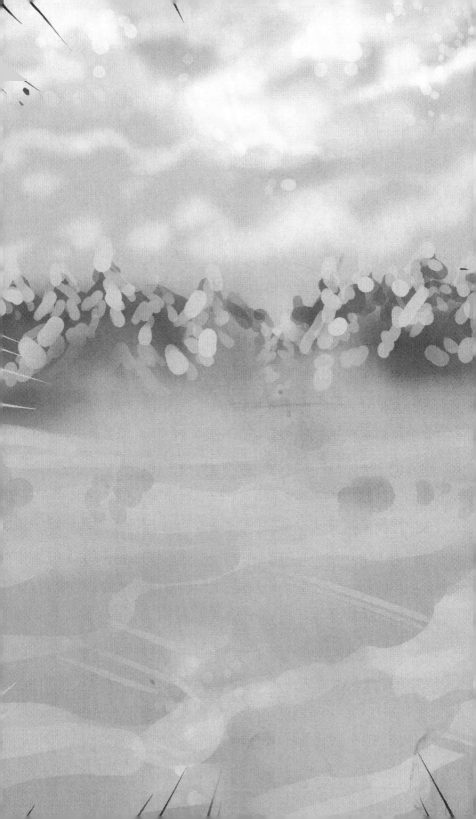

# 12

IT WAS FIVE minutes after the last bell and Cameron was still pacing the student pick-up area of the parking lot. Usually he took the bus home, or caught a ride with one of his friends, but not on Fridays. On Fridays his mom worked an overnight shift at the hospital and that meant she had just enough time to pick Cameron up from school before she had to shower and start getting ready. It was something they both enjoyed, especially since the ride home was the only time she'd get to spend with her son until she woke up late Saturday afternoon. (Apparently going to sleep at four in the morning took a lot out of you.) She never complained about it though, which was one of the many things Cameron admired about her.

Cameron was so distracted by his thoughts that he missed his mom's signature honk. She had to do it again, earning both her and her son some weird looks. Cameron shook his head clear and walked over, climbing into the front seat and fastening his seatbelt.

Out of the side of his eyes, Cameron could see his mom frowning at him.

"Everything okay, kiddo?" she asked, effortlessly turning onto the main road.

Cameron sighed and slumped down in the seat.

"Yeah, I'm just a little nervous about the game is all."

His mom smiled kindly.

"I'd tell you to stop worrying and just have fun if I thought it'd make a difference."

Cameron laughed.

"Thanks, mom," he said, and he meant it. Maybe it wasn't always the coolest thing for your mom to know everything about you, but it sure was comforting in times like these. They made it through the rest of the drive in comfortable silence.

At home, Cameron gave his mom a big hug and the two of them disappeared into separate rooms to get ready. Unlike Millie, who kept everything thrown about her mess of a room, Cameron already had his gear packed up and ready to go. All he needed to do was change. He stripped down and carefully pulled on his hockey pants, pads, and jersey. He finished the look with his hockey socks and kept his skates, gloves, and helmet in the bag for later when he'd actually need them. He dragged both the bag and his stick back to the living room where he sat down on the couch and waited for Luke's mom to come pick him up.

Cameron couldn't stop thinking about the game and what winning it would feel like. He knew it was terrible, and that his mom would be disappointed in him for thinking this way, but he wanted to win not so that he could feel good about himself, but so that Millie would feel bad for leaving him. He wasn't exactly sure what the word petty meant, but he was pretty sure it was something like this.

He didn't have too long to think about it, though. Before he knew it, his ride was there and he was rushing out the door.

Millie walked through the woods to get to the pond like she always did. People were always telling her to be careful and that she was too young to always be going places by herself, but she knew these woods like the back of her hands. It was impossible for her to get lost in here, and even when she was all the way at the pond, she was still close enough to town that someone would hear her if she screamed.

She knew that she was probably one of the last players to arrive, but she just couldn't force herself to rush. She needed this bit of quiet to get in the zone. This was her moment. This was her chance to prove to everyone, including herself, how great of a captain she really was. It was going to be amazing.

Just as the pond and all of the neighborhood kids gathered around it came into view, someone came up behind Millie and tapped her on the shoulder. She almost jumped out of her skin before realizing it was just her cousin.

"Jeez, Logan," she hissed. "Don't do that!"

"Sorry," Logan said, holding his hands in the air. "I just wanted to talk to you for a second before we go out there."

"Talk to me about what?" Millie asked, confused.

"Well, I just wanted to make sure you were okay? You seem so...um...aggressive these days and I..."

Millie rolled her eyes.

"Stop using big words, Log."

Logan rolled his eyes right back. The gesture made it very easy to see that they were related.

"I *mean* that you've been acting really weird and I want to make sure we're okay, and that you're not going to let whatever happens in this game decide how you treat all of us for the rest of the year."

Millie sighed and rubbed her face with her free hand.

"Logan. We're family. Of course we're okay.

And I just want to win, okay? That's all. Same way anyone would. Same way you do. Now stop trying to freak me out."

Logan looked like he wanted to argue, but eventually he just shrugged his shoulders and ran out to join his team. Millie closed her eyes and counted to thirty before doing the same.

It was time for the game to begin.

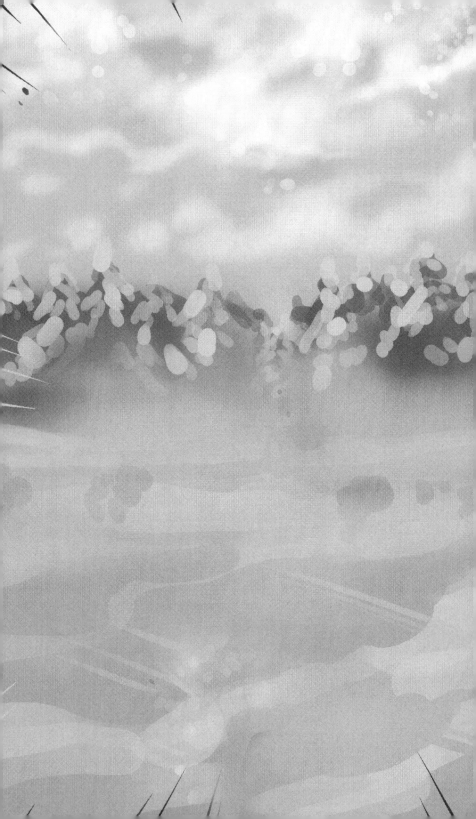

# 13

AFTER ALL THE kids were accounted for, Jon pulled the boys aside for a quick pep talk and Bev did the same for the girls. The two teens' speeches were nearly identical, with each of them focusing on how hard the kids had worked and how important it was to focus that energy into the game while still having fun with it.

Their words of encouragement seemed to work. There wasn't a single frown in sight out on the ice. The kids all believed with all of their hearts that they had everything it took to crush their competition. All friendships, crushes, and grudges were temporarily put on hold for the sake of playing the best possible game.

Each team was given a quick ten-minute warm-up, which was a lot of pressure for Millie and Cameron, who weren't used to calling the shots in front of such a large audience. Apparently the pond kids weren't the only ones who were tempted by a good old-fashioned battle of the sexes. Not only had pretty much the entire fourth-grade class shown up, but also most of the third and fifth graders, and even some sixth graders as well.

There were already some of the Thunder and Lightning's usual fan chants filling the air, not to mention the half dozen or so kids holding up cell phones and tablets to record all the action for those not lucky enough to be able to sneak away and watch the game for themselves.

Millie spent most of her warm-up time skating laps around the perimeter of the pond and trying her best to block out the noise and faces all around her. Khloe was looking comfortable in goal, all padded up and doing her usual stretches. Ashlyn and Daylyn were passing pucks back and forth, while Georgia and Lola were circling the empty goalpost and taking turns making shots. Violet still seemed kind of out of it, but at least she was up on her feet and skating. Sage was a little preoccupied with taping her stick, but Millie didn't bother arguing with her about it. It was just part of her pregame ritual or whatever.

Cameron took a slightly more hands-on approach to his team's warm-up. He had all the boys line up side by side and skate three laps around the pond. Then they all took turns shooting on Logan and finished with some group stretching. Before he knew it, the whistle was blown and he and Millie were being called to center ice for the opening faceoff.

Cameron was nervous, but much less so than Millie. Back when they were friends, he was always the one to calm her down and help her get her head in the game. Glancing up at her now though, he didn't think anyone else could really tell from the outside how flustered she was. The only dead giveaway was the small crease down the middle of her forehead.

Millie, despite her nerves, wasn't thinking

about Cameron at all, and she was only half-listening as Jon went over the game's stakes and rules for the assembled crowd. She had her knees bent and her body low to the ice. Her eyes were focused solely on the puck in Bev's hands. That puck was going to be hers, and she knew exactly what she was going to do once she got it. She was going to send it wide for Georgia, who would hopefully carry it all the way up the ice and make a goal.

Unfortunately for her, the Lightning D-men didn't seem to like that plan very much. After the puck was dropped Millie did manage to pass to Georgia as planned. Georgia barely made it into the offensive zone before Ben and Linkin boxed her in, forcing her to drop the puck for Daylyn, who overskated it and had to fumble backwards to make a clumsy recovery. Daylyn brought the puck around behind the goal in an attempt to catch her breath, but that didn't work either. Hunter immediately swooped in and wrestled the puck away, quickly sending it up to Cameron who batted it in before Khloe could get into position.

The whistle sounded. The goal was called, and Millie angrily skated over to the edge of the ice to get some water. About a third of the crowd was shouting "Girls stink!" at her as she adjusted her helmet and went back out to center ice.

This time, Millie focused less intently on the puck, and more on her anger over being bested. She channeled that into her playing and barreled right through Cameron after winning the faceoff, not bothering to pass the puck to anyone else. The boys were so surprised by this move that it took them a moment to switch gears and come after her. By then she was already staring Logan down and aiming for his weak spot.

In a matter of seconds she had tied the game. The crowd was going wild and Millie's heart was beating out of her chest.

"Take that," she whispered at no one in particular.

Cameron heard her, but didn't respond, mostly because it was hard to frown (or show any emotion, really) with his mouthguard in.

The game proceeded in this fashion for most of the first period. Any time one of the teams scored, the other team scored right back. It was impossible for anyone to get a solid lead because they were just so evenly matched. It was a good thing the audience was standing, because if they weren't, they'd be stuck on the edge of their seats.

And then the snow started falling.

It wasn't that big of a deal at first, just a light flurry; easy enough to ignore. Then the wind picked up and the snowfall became heavy enough to start sticking to the ground. By this point, it was barely halfway through the second period, but already the audience was clearing out fast.

The kids refused to be stopped, though. They didn't care who was watching. This was personal. This was about bragging rights. They would gladly play all night in a blizzard if it meant they could finally determine a winner.

But Jon and Bev weren't having it. It hadn't even been snowing for twenty minutes and it was already getting harder to see. Plus, they didn't quite feel like delivering a bunch of little kid-sicles to sixteen sets of angry parents later that evening.

Jon blew the whistle and declared that they would have to reschedule, much to the players' dismay.

"Come on, man," Rhys whined. "The game's almost over. It's not snowing *that* hard. We can still play."

Then he completely disproved his point by falling flat on his butt.

"Another time, kiddo," said Bev as Linkin and Preston carefully helped him up. "Everyone change back into your street shoes. I'm gonna go call your parents and tell them to come pick you up."

This time nobody argued. They could all sense the finality in Bev's words. They robotically packed up their stuff and allowed Jon to lead them over to Mrs. Jefferson's covered porch to wait. A few minutes later, he left them alone to go help Bev make phone calls. The kids huddled close for warmth and stared out at the billowing snow.

"This blows," Daylyn said, finally breaking the silence.

The kids all expressed their agreement.

"All of that fuss over nothing," Preston added.

"I feel gypped," said Lola.

"Me too," Ben nodded.

"What are we supposed to do now?" Hunter asked.

Cameron shrugged. "Wait another week and do it all over again, I guess."

"Are you kidding?" Ashlyn asked, outraged. "We all barely made it through this week."

"Yeah," said Georgia. "We're gonna rip each other's heads off."

"Violet and Linkin already got in trouble once for fighting," Millie said softly.

The kids all glanced at the pair in question. It was the first time since the incident that any of them had tried addressing the elephant in the room. Violet and Linkin were looking at each other very intensely; almost as if they were having a silent conversation. Finally they nodded at each other, seeming to have reached an agreement.

"We didn't actually get in trouble for fighting," Linkin said, surprising them all. He felt so relieved to finally be able to say it out loud.

"What do you mean?" Luke asked, confused.

"Yeah." Khloe crossed her arms and narrowed her eyes. "If it wasn't fighting, what *did* you get called into the office for?"

Violet's cheeks were already quite pink due to the cold, but they somehow managed to get even pinker as she said, "PDA."

"What does that even mean?" asked Ben.

"Public display of affection," Sage informed him. "Like kissing and stuff."

"YOU TWO WERE KISSING?" Rhys asked, appalled. He wanted to throw up just at the thought. Sooooo disgusting.

"No!" Linkin and Violet shouted as one.

"We weren't kissing," Violet said. "But we do..."

"Like each other," Linkin finished with a sigh.

The rest of them looked back and forth

between the happy couple as if they'd both just sprouted new heads. All except for Logan, who hissed the words, "I knew it!" under his breath.

"Well, congratulations, I guess," Ashlyn said, patting Violet on the back.

Millie opened and closed her mouth a couple of times without really knowing what to say. She knew she should be happy for her friend, but she was just so freaking confused. This was by far one of the weirdest things that had ever happened to her.

Luckily, her parents chose that exact moment to pull up to Mrs. Jefferson's driveway and honk. Millie started to make her way down the porch steps just as her dad rolled down the passenger window and stuck his head out.

"Logan, Cameron," he shouted. "You're with us."

Millie and Cameron took a moment to stare at each other as Logan raced ahead of them down the driveway.

As if this day could get any worse.

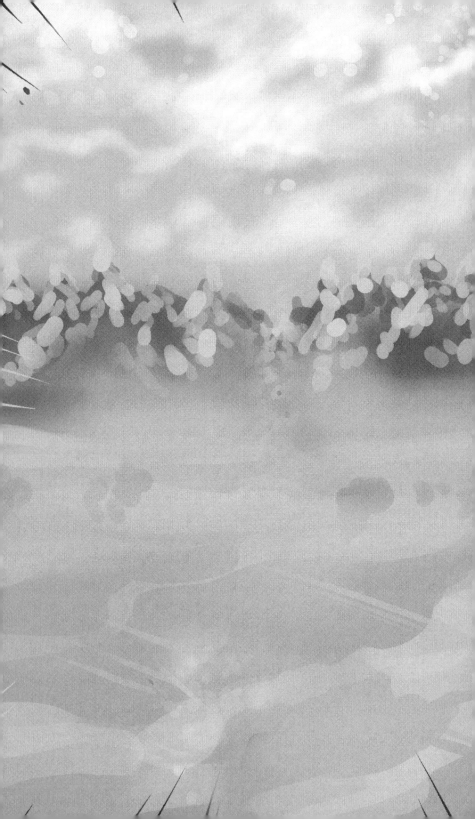

# 14

THE THREE CHILDREN were crammed into the back seat of the car with Logan between Millie and Cameron, both of whom were refusing to look at each other. Logan didn't seem to mind. He just kept animatedly talking to Millie's parents and telling them about school and how the game had been going before they'd shut everything down. As usual, he spared none of the details. Thus, when her mom finally pulled up to Logan's apartment complex, Millie was more than a little bit relieved, even if it did leave her alone with Cameron.

"Thanks for the ride, Aunt Patty," Logan said, unbuckling his seatbelt. "See you, Uncle Brian."

"Bye, kiddo. Be good," Millie's mom said to him, waving in the rearview mirror.

Millie had to momentarily step out of the car so that Logan could get out. When she sat back down, that was when everything went from bad to worse.

"Cameron, honey," her mom was saying, "your dad called to let us know that he's working overtime because of the snowstorm. He probably won't be able to make it home until tomorrow, and since your mom's stuck at the hospital, it looks like you're gonna have to stay with us for tonight."

"What?" Millie shouted in outrage. She thought they were just dropping Cameron off.

"Millie Anne," her father said in a warning tone. He only ever used her full name when he really meant business.

"It's just for one night," her mother assured.

"It's cool," Cameron said with a shrug, even though it was not cool. It was very *uncool*, in fact. On this he and Millie could agree. They rode the rest of the way in silence.

By the time they finally reached Millie's block, they were inching along at a snail's pace due to the storm. They could barely see out the windows as they swung into the driveway. Millie's dad lifted his hood and gripped his house key tightly in his hand.

"Ready to make a run for it?" he asked.

Millie and Cameron nodded and the four of them got out and ran for the porch. Her dad fumbled with the key once, but managed to get it in on the second try. The kids dropped their gear on the floor and they all stood by the door for a few minutes, peeling off their coats and boots. Then Millie's dad kissed his wife on the cheek before returning to his downstairs office. After he disappeared from sight, Millie's mom turned to face the kids.

"Okay. Who wants hot chocolate?" she asked.

"Me!" said Millie.

"Yes, please," Cameron agreed.

Patty smiled kindly, appreciating how much the kids loved her hot chocolate.

"Okay, why don't you two go wait in the living room and get warmed up."

Millie and Cameron nodded and did as they were asked. There was really no point arguing. They were stuck with each other for the night. The house was pretty big, but not so big that they could just disappear into separate rooms and not speak to each other. And even if that were an option, Millie's parents certainly wouldn't allow it. Her parents would say she was being selfish and rude, and she'd never hear the end of it.

Not for the first time, she wondered what her parents really thought about her and Cameron's little feud. Certainly, her parents had noticed that the two of them rarely spent any time together anymore and that when she did speak of him, she did so with an angry pout to her lips.

It had to be weird for them, and for Cameron's parents as well. They were all still "thick as thieves," as her grandpa would say, although she didn't quite know why thieves would be considered thick. It sounded a whole lot like a fat joke to her, but it was aimed at criminals, so she guessed it couldn't be *that* mean.

Shaking her head, Millie plopped down on the patterned rug in the middle of the living room, yanked off her slightly damp socks, and splayed out in front of the fireplace to warm her feet. Cameron walked automatically to the front-facing window and drew back the long blue curtains before coming to join her. They sat in silence for several minutes and watched the storm continue to roll in. For a moment, it was just like old times. Millie found herself starting to relax against her will. She kind of hated that even after everything that had gone down between them, Cameron still had such a calming effect on her.

"It's weird, right?" Cameron said finally, breaking the silence. "Linkin and Violet."

Millie nodded her head.

"Super weird."

"Like, I mean, I want them to be happy and everything, but it's just like..."

"Gross?" Millie offered.

Cameron cringed but nodded anyway.

"Yeah. It's a little gross," he admitted. "I guess I've just always thought of you girls as family. Clearly Linkin doesn't feel the same way."

Millie snorted and Cameron's face lit up with recognition. It'd been such a long time since he'd heard her laugh like that. Millie just sort of sat there uncomfortably, cheeks red. Even though Cameron had been joking around, it was hard to miss the nugget of truth nestled behind his words. Somewhere, deep deep down, he still thought of Millie as family.

She felt like she should call him out on it, but the words died on her lips as her mom showed up with two steaming hot mugs which she sat down in front of them before returning to the kitchen to get started on dinner.

Cameron reached for one of the mugs and held it firmly in both hands.

"I feel pretty bad about it honestly," he went on without missing a beat.

"What do you mean?" Millie asked, confused.

She rolled over onto her belly and propped herself up on her elbows to look at him.

Cameron took a careful sip of the hot cocoa and then cleared his throat.

"Well, I'm pretty sure the only reason Link and Vi were keeping things secret was because of us. Like, they felt obligated not to betray their teams or something."

Millie scrunched her eyebrows together and reached for her mug. She hadn't thought of it that way. As usual, she'd been too caught up in her own feelings to care.

"That's just great," she complained. "Now I feel guilty too."

Cameron gave her a small smile and Millie gave him one right back, and before long the two of them had lapsed into the most comfortable silence they'd had in a long time.

That night, Cameron laid sprawled out on Millie's bedroom floor with the blow up mattress, pillows and an old t-shirt quilt that Millie's dad had dug out for him. It felt incredibly weird to be doing this again, and yet, that didn't stop him from enjoying the familiar creaking noises the house made as the wind whistled outside, or the soft hum of the TV downstairs, or the way Millie's rapid breathing told him that she was still awake, no matter how hard she was trying to pretend otherwise.

He rolled over onto his side so that he was looking up at the side of her shadowed face.

"Hey, Mills?" he asked quietly.

Millie popped one eye open and glanced down at him.

"Yeah?"

Cameron took a deep breath and prepared himself to say the words he should have said a long time ago.

"I think I owe you an apology."

The springs creaked as Millie shifted her weight in bed.

"I'm not saying I disagree," she began, "but for what exactly?"

"Well, for everything really. I shouldn't have let things get this bad between us."

Millie was quiet for a long time and Cameron worried that she may have actually fallen asleep. Then she said, voice small, "Why did you, then?"

Cameron rubbed at the bridge of his nose in the way his dad sometimes did when he got stressed out. The motion didn't provide as much comfort as he'd hoped it would.

"I was jealous," he admitted. It actually felt pretty good to finally say it out loud.

The whites of Millie's eyes shone brightly in the shadowy room as if they were popping right out of her skull.

"Jealous?" she asked incredulously. "Why?"

Cameron gave a little shrug.

"I felt like you were leaving me behind. That you didn't want to be on my team anymore because you had Lola and Georgia and the rest of the girls."

Millie felt something in her mind snap into place. Suddenly all of Cameron's actions over the last couple of months made a lot of sense. She felt like a horrible friend. He'd been hurting all this time and she hadn't even known.

"I'm sorry," she whispered, surprised to find a rare tear spilling from her eye.

"Don't be," he said. "It's not your fault that I acted like a jerk."

"You should have told me..." Millie trailed off.

"I know." Cameron chewed on his bottom lip. "You just seemed so much happier without me."

Millie sat up and shook her head fiercely.

"Cameron. That isn't even a little bit true. You wanna know why I really left for the Hurricanes?"

"Why?"

"Because I was trying to be more like you."

Cameron let out a choking laugh that sounded way too loud in the stillness of the night.

"So what you're saying is that we're both idiots and we've been mad at each other for no reason?"

"Pretty much," Millie agreed. "So where do we go from here?"

Cameron sat up so that they could both see each other's face.

"Do you forgive me?"

"Yes," Millie said without hesitation. "Do you forgive me?"

Cameron nodded and wiped his tears on his sleeve.

"In that case," he said quietly. "I think it's time for us to make a truce."

# 15

***One month later***

"OKAY," BEN HUFFED, hunched over to catch his breath. "You two shouldn't be allowed to be on the same team."

Cameron just laughed and gave Millie a high five.

"You snooze, you lose," she said, feeling smug. She'd just pulled off a perfect one-timer with Cameron on the assist, stunning everyone, including herself.

On the weekends down at the rec center the Hurricanes and Lightning were still two very separate entities, but during the week it was all about practicing some killer moves and having fun. Not to mention crushing the competition: co-ed teams or not, they were all still hockey players. They wanted to win.

Which really sucked for whoever happened to get stuck playing against Millie and Cameron, who'd been an unstoppable force from the moment they first made up. Since their reunion, it was like all of the friction between the two teams had just melted away. Linkin and Violet were always making eyes at each other and holding hands when they thought no one was looking. Lola and Ben were working on a comic strip together, something having to do with a large poop-themed superhero that Millie had been too scared to ask about. Khloe and Logan were constantly off talking about weird goalie things that sounded like gibberish to everyone else, and Ashlyn was tutoring at least three of the boys in math.

Things were good. Better than good, even. It felt as though everything was just as it should be. As of now, there were no official plans to reschedule the boys-versus-girls battle for the ice. They all agreed that it was much more fun playing together. It was like having your cake and eating it too, as Millie's grandpa would say.

Also, Cameron. It was amazing playing on a team with him again. It just felt right, like she could finally take a breath after months and months of holding it in. The best part was that she could tell without asking that Cameron felt exactly the same way.

They were all growing and changing and turning into the people they were meant to be, but they weren't grown up yet. They still had plenty of time to play together, and Millie intended to make the most of that time—but looking out across the ice at all of her friends' smiling faces, she had to admit.

Some things were even more important than hockey.

# HOCKEY WARS

## THE NEW GIRL

## TURN THE PAGE FOR A SNEAK PEEK

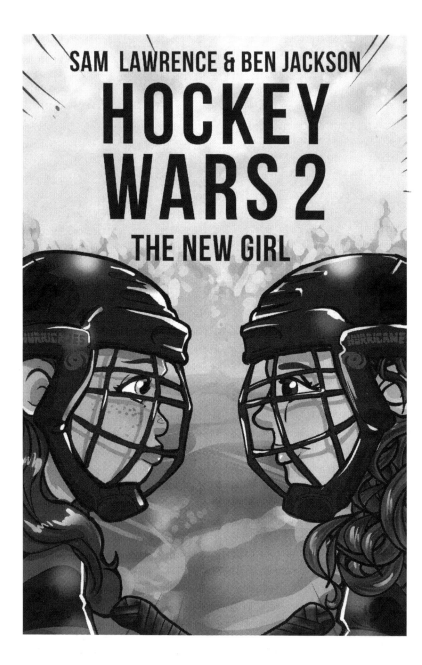

# 1

MILLIE AND THE other girls from her team were sitting around with Cameron and a few of the other boys from the boys' team, stretching and chatting while both teams waited for their field lacrosse game to start. It was almost the end of the field lacrosse season, and both the boys' and girls' teams were playing on the same field for once.

Usually, they played on opposite sides of town, on different days and at different times. It was nice to be able to hang out together between games and relax. Some of the parents had brought a BBQ and food, and a tailgate party had popped up in the carpark.

Soon summer would be over, and the long

hot days would be gone, but it wasn't all bad news. The end of summer meant the start of something else: hockey! Lacrosse was fun, but hockey was everyone's favorite sport, and both the boys and girls were hoping to have an amazing season this year. The girls had a real shot at taking the championship.

As the girls waited for their game to start, they talked about who they were playing in their last lacrosse game of the regular season coming up next weekend. The Baxter Panthers. *Bleh*. They all knew they didn't have a chance. The Panthers had smashed them earlier in the season, and the next game would probably be much the same.

Unfortunately, they weren't going to make it into the field lacrosse finals this year. Neither team had managed to put together a great season in the win department, but they'd all had a blast playing and hoped that next year they would come out a lot stronger.

"OMG! You won't believe what I heard my mom talking about with your mom, V!" Daylyn blurted out as she came running up to where the two teams were lounging around.

Concern and confusion flashed across Violet's face as she waited for Daylyn to finish speaking.

"Well, what is it, Daylyn?"

"Apparently, the coaches are making some big announcement at tonight's preseason meeting," blurted out Daylyn, not able to hold it in any longer.

"Aaand...what's this big announcement?" Millie asked impatiently. Just once it would be nice if Daylyn could get to the point without turning everything into a total drama.

"Day, come on. We already knew that. They sent all of our parents that email. Remember?" Georgia said, just a little bit confused about the whole thing.

"What I think they're all asking you, Day, is what did you hear exactly? What's the big news?" laughed Cameron. *Girls*, Cameron thought, *everything has to be a big production.* "Get to the point already!"

"If you would all stop talking for just one minute, I would tell you!" huffed Daylyn, crossing her arms and pouting. "As I was trying to say before all of you so rudely interrupted me, I totally overheard my mom say that the coaches are introducing a new girl to our team tonight!" Daylyn said, trying to get it all out before someone else interrupted.

"OMG!" they all said in unison. This wasn't good news. Chaos erupted as all the girls tried to speak over each other.

"We already have a full team?"

"Where is the new girl going to play?"

"What position will she play?"

"Will one of us lose our spot?"

"We already had tryouts. I'm not losing my spot!"

Cameron stood up and looked around at the other boys, motioning them to follow him. "WOW," he mouthed silently, looking around as the other boys followed his lead and stood up as well, moving away from the girls who were now all huddled together.

"Umm, that was totally intense," Hunter said as the boys looked over at the girls who were now wildly waving their hands around.

"You're telling me, buddy," Cameron replied.

"I wonder if she's cute?" Luke asked.

"You wish!" Logan said, ducking away as Luke tried to grab him in a headlock.

A siren sounded, announcing the end of the games currently underway out on the field.

"All right, guys, we have to go out and warm up. Get your gear and meet me down at the far end of the field. Luke, you start them stretching, and I'll be there in a minute," Cameron said as he picked up his lacrosse stick and started walking towards where Millie sat with the other girls, who were all still losing their minds. The boys nodded and started jogging down to the far end of the field.

"Mills?" Cameron called out as he walked towards her. "Mills!"

"What!? I mean, umm, what, Cam?" Millie asked, still trying to hear what the other girls were talking about.

"The siren just went."

"So, what? Oh, crap! Right! Thanks! I owe you!"

"No worries," Cameron said, laughing as he walked away shaking his head. Girls. Just when you think you've got them all figured out you learn something new. Who would have thought that getting a new player would cause so much chaos? At least his team wasn't getting any new players this season.

"Okay, girls! Grab your gear and get out on the field. We only have a few minutes to warm up!" Millie shouted, panicking, as she looked around for her lacrosse stick.

"I wonder if the new girl plays center?" Khloe shouted as she struggled to put her goalie pads on, watching a horrified expression come over Millie's face.

"I heard she was a goalie!" Violet shouted back with a big grin on her face.

"Shut up! There is no way!" Khloe looked horrified.

"Enough! We have a game to play. Let's

worry about the new girl after we finish this game. Let's go, team, long lap. Let's go!" Millie shouted, leading her team on a run around the outside of the field.

It was easy enough to say it, Millie thought, but what if the new girl did play center, and what if she was good? Millie knew that she was good—that's why she was the captain—but there was always a little doubt that someone could come along and steal her spot away from her. *Enough!* Millie thought as the team ran around the field. *Focus on today's game; worry about the rest later.*

**Third Book in the Series Out Now**

# NOTE FROM THE AUTHORS

As Indie authors, we work hard to produce high-quality work for the enjoyment of all of our readers. If you can spare one minute just to leave a short review of our book, we would greatly appreciate it!

Let everyone know just how much you and your children enjoyed *Hockey Wars*!

We are currently working on expanding this series so stay tuned for future updates by following us on Facebook or visit our website!

www.facebook.com/benandsamauthors

&

www.benandsamauthors.com

Thank you, Ben and Sam ☺

Made in the USA
Columbia, SC
09 January 2020